This book belongs to

_____

_____

_____

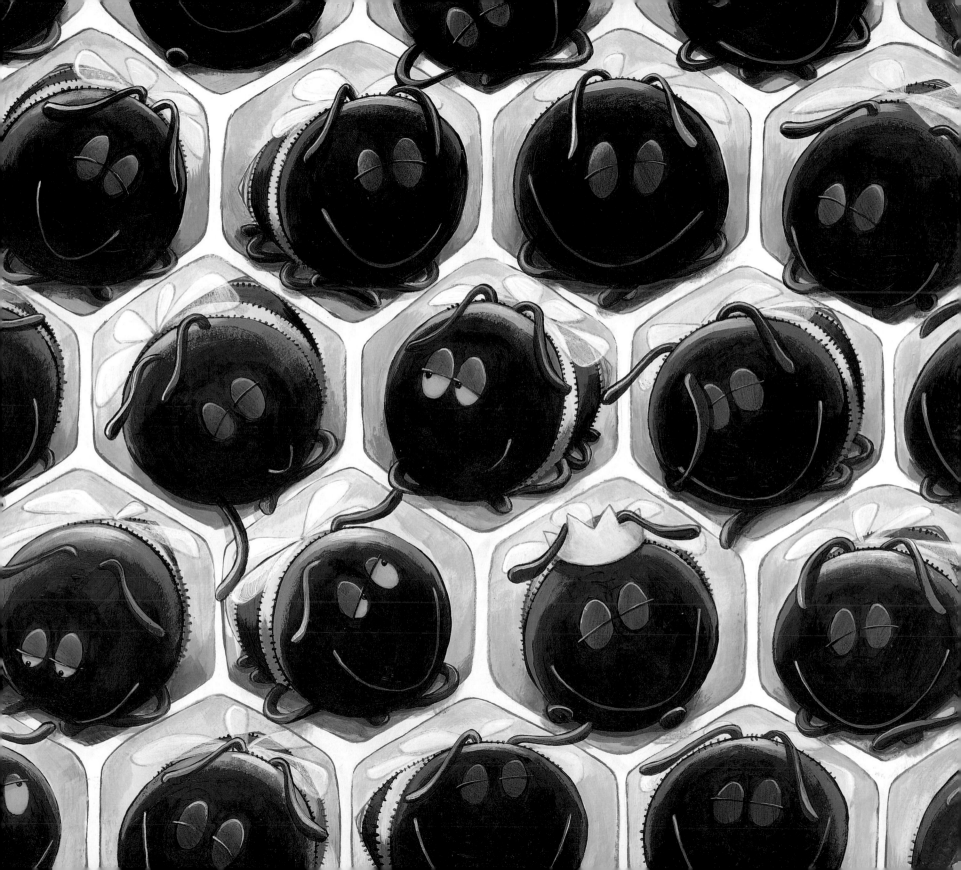

For Sam, who taught me
everything I know about bees
–S.S.

For my BEEootiful baBEE, Levi
–J.T.

tiger tales
an imprint of ME Media, LLC
202 Old Ridgefield Road, Wilton, CT 06897
This paperback edition published 2010
First published in the United States 2007
Originally published in Great Britain 2007
by Little Tiger Press
an imprint of Magi Publications
Text copyright © 2007 Steve Smallman
Illustrations copyright © 2007 Jack Tickle
CIP data is available
ISBN-13: 978-1-58925-065-9 (hardcover)
ISBN-10: 1-58925-065-6 (hardcover)
ISBN-13: 978-1-58925-422-0 (paperback)
ISBN-10: 1-58925-422-8 (paperback)
Printed in China
LPP0709

The Very Greedy Bee

by Steve Smallman   Illustrated by Jack Tickle

tiger tales

In a busy, buzzy beehive lived a very greedy bee. All the other bees worked hard making honey and cleaning the hive, but the greedy bee spent all day gobbling pollen and guzzling nectar.

SLURP! SLURP! BURP!

The greedy bee wouldn't share his nectar with anyone.

He wouldn't even let a tired ladybug sit on his flower.

"Find your own flower!" he shouted. "This one is **MINE!**"

And when, one day, the greedy bee found a meadow full of the biggest, juiciest flowers he had ever seen, he decided not to tell **ANYONE**!

"**YUMMY**!" he buzzed. "Lots and lots of flowers and they're all for **ME**!"

The greedy bee whizzed and bizzed from flower to flower, slurping and burping and growing **FATTER**...

and **FATTER**...

and **FATTER** ...

and **FATTER!**

At last, his tummy
was full and he settled
down on a big pink
flower in the warm
yellow sunshine and
fell fast asleep.

ZZZZZZZZZZ!

When the greedy bee woke
up, it was **DARK**. He tried to fly,
but his tummy was so roly and
poly that...

BIFF!

BANG!

THUMP!

he went down instead of up
and crashed—**BIFF! BANG!
THUMP!**—to the ground.

"**I'M SCARED**!" cried the greedy bee. "And I don't know how to get home!"

Then he saw two glowing eyes in the long grass.

"**EEK!**" he cried. "**A MONSTER** is coming to eat me!"

But it wasn't a monster. It was two friendly
fireflies, their bottoms glowing in the dark.
"What's wrong?" they asked.
"I'm too full to fly," wailed the greedy bee,
"and I can't walk home in the dark!"

"Follow us," said the fireflies, and they all
set off on the long, long journey home.

Through forests
of flowers and
squishy mud...

over the hills and under the
stars trudged the greedy
bee. He had never walked so
far and he was very tired.

"Nearly there!"
called the fireflies.

Then they heard
the **WHOOSH** of
rushing water....

"I'm almost home!" cried the greedy
bee excitedly. "It's the stream!"
    And it was, but his hive was on the
other side of it.

"Oh no," said the greedy bee, sadly flopping down on the grass. "How will I ever get across?"

"We'll help you!" said a tiny ant with a big leaf.

The ant and his friends flipped
the big leaf into the water.
"Jump on!" they cried.
Helped by the fireflies, the
greedy bee and the ants made their
way splishing and splashing to the
other side of the stream.

"**HOORAY! I'M HOME**!" cheered the greedy bee.

"Where have you been?" asked the other bees.

"I **OVERSLURPED**!" said the greedy bee. "I would never
have made it home if my new friends hadn't been so kind.
Now I'm going to share my best honey
with them. Would you like some, too?"

"Yes!" said the other bees. "Let's have a party!"

Everyone enjoyed
a midnight feast of
yummy, runny honey.
All except for one very
sleepy, very happy, but
NOT so greedy bee!

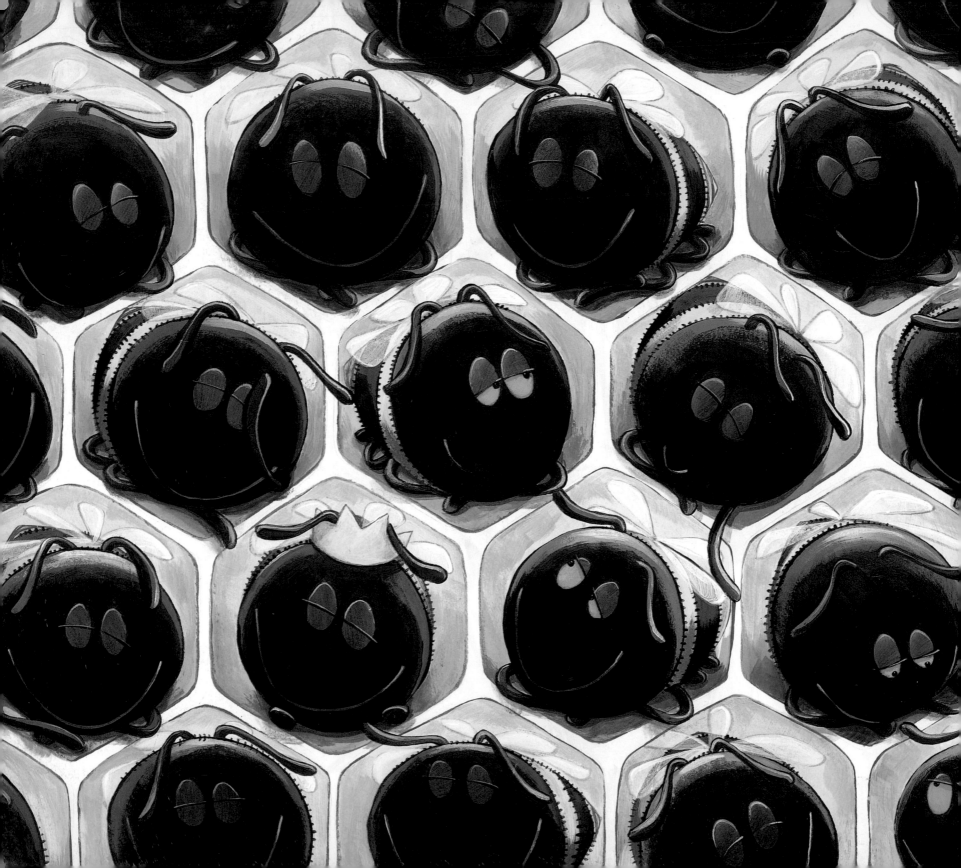

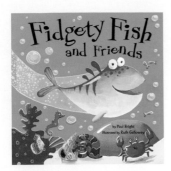

Fidgety Fish and Friends
by Paul Bright
Illustrated by Ruth Galloway
ISBN-13: 978-1-58925-409-1
ISBN-10: 1-58925-409-0

The Very Ugly Bug
by Liz Pichon
ISBN-13: 978-1-58925-404-6
ISBN-10: 1-58925-404-X

Itsy Bitsy Spider
by Keith Chapman
Illustrated by Jack Tickle
ISBN-13: 978-1-58925-407-7
ISBN-10: 1-58925-407-4

The 108th Sheep
by Ayano Imai
ISBN-13: 978-1-58925-420-6
ISBN-10: 1-58925-420-1

Explore the world of tiger tales!

More fun-filled and exciting stories await you!
Look for these titles and more at your local library or bookstore.
And have fun reading!

tiger tales

202 Old Ridgefield Road, Wilton, CT 06897

Good Night, Sleep Tight!
by Claire Freedman
Illustrated by Rory Tyger
ISBN-13: 978-1-58925-405-3
ISBN-10: 1-58925-405-8

Boris and the Snoozebox
by Leigh Hodgkinson
ISBN-13: 978-1-58925-421-3
ISBN-10: 1-58925-421-X

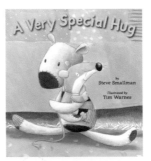

A Very Special Hug
by Steve Smallman
Illustrated by Tim Warnes
ISBN-13: 978-1-58925-410-7
ISBN-10: 1-58925-410-4

Just for You!
by Christine Leeson
Illustrated by Andy Ellis
ISBN-13: 978-1-58925-408-4
ISBN-10: 1-58925-408-2